OBSIDIAN

Tales of Karanga

Mike McCoy

ISBN: 978-1-7366021-2-6 (e-book)
         978-1-7366021-3-3 (paperback)
         978-1-7366021-4-0 (IngramSpark Paperback)

First Edition
Published by Blaster Tech in the United States of America
Updated March 2024

Blaster Tech
Cerritos, CA. 90703

OBSIDIAN
Tales of Karanga

Chapter ONE

I follow a monotonous routine repeated for an eternity.

My pod cover slides back with a whoosh. I reach down without looking and pull out the long umbilical tube. I stand, step out of my pod, and walk to the hot sand bath. There's nothing more pleasing than digging deep and rolling in the warm sand to scrub away five spans of dead skin, sweat, and yuck.

I walk up the steps, zombie-like, to the flight deck, grab a fist full of chika, and swallow them whole.

It's Banga or Raviro, my shipmates, who greet me. Sometimes I pull a double so I can see Raviro, even if it's only for a few minutes. She's usually in a better mood than Banga. There's never anything to report, so whoever is going off shift walks past like a shadow eager to get below deck and into their pod. Hibernation relieves boredom.

Alone again, I move through our small dark vessel. Dimmed lights burn yellow against the black walls and floor.

I mechanically shuffle through my daily chores. The repetition of my duties are burned into my being. Check the power reserve. Grab the bucket of condensate that drips from the limb at the aft of the vessel and pour it into the water tank. Fill the feeding reservoir. Our waste feeds them. The chika must eat. Separate six sets of mature ones for breeding. If the young are big enough, dump them in the storage bin. Gulp down another handful of the squirming grubs, then tidy things up. Raviro keeps a tight ship. Banga is the messy one. The rest of the day is for my idle pleasure.

Without a clock to mark the passing of days and increment the spans, I would have no concept of time, for there is no night nor daylight. Our ship has no view ports. The forward display can project recorded battle sequences, but the eyes that brought outside views to the ship's walls are blinded and the hatch, our only exit, won't open.

At random times, the water bucket fills faster, the volume of drips exceeds what condensate normally produces. These are rare, exciting days. The excess water is a blessing. It keeps us alive. Raviro says it's Mwari watching over us. I'm not so sure.

I dutifully complete my daily chores, sleep when tired, eat when hungry, and keep watch until my shift of five spans is complete, hibernate, repeat. This is the dreary cycle we have followed for thousands of spans.

We keep watch. We have hope.

The only other choice is to die. I agreed long ago to not accept that fate. We live for a warrior's death. We will not defile the honor of our families by taking our lives like weak Scraggs, even if no one will ever know. Raviro says we must be strong and have faith, but even she must concede that no one will ever find us. Regardless, we have agreed to carry on. I have time, endless time. While it ticks slowly past, I endeavor to write the saga of how we came to be here. I write for myself, knowing no other being will read this.

My name is Majaya Masimba Gwinyai. I am Karanga. We are a noble, powerful people. Karanga have tended the gardens, forests, and oceans of these lush lands since time began. My first name means brothers. I am the second son born in a single span. Our people considered my birth a great blessing to my family and a sign to all karanga that the power my father wielded was great, for it is exceedingly rare that a man produces two sons in a single span.

I prefer my middle name, Masimba. It means powerful. As a boy, I dreamed of growing tall and strong like my father, doing great deeds, winning battles, achieving victory. My middle name fits well with our family name, Gwinyai, which means strength. I am powerful strength. I like that. It's much better than second brother. My brethren call me Mas Gwinyai.

We are ancient. Karanga have nurtured the gardens since the dawn of time. Over millennia, we learned to use the power that builds majestic mountains and put it to good purpose making metal. We conquered the mystery of the sky, capturing its storm power when it touches our steel. Once we learned to harness energy from the skies, karanga used it to make the lives of our people better. We learned to use the wind and the power of the sky to rise over the garden and view it from above. Like birds and butterflies, we soar through the air in wondrous vessels.

The karanga prospered, but we never forsook our primary role. Our essential purpose is working to keep nature in balance, for our garden is a beautiful green, blue paradise spinning slowly through the galaxy, and we must preserve it forever. We used knowledge and power to care for the garden and the rivers living in harmony with nature, for it is the air, trees, and water that nurture us.

But not everything in the garden should be allowed to live. When weeds infest the garden, stealing nutrients, spreading wide, crowding out the harvest, do you not cull the weeds? Karanga are peaceful beings. We knew the Scragg were out there. We left them alone. They weren't hurting us; the elders said. Their existence is Mwari's will, said others. When weeds in the garden are sparse, you may dismiss them. Our tolerance allowed the weed to grow.

The Scragg do not tend the garden; they strip it bare. Wherever they go, they kill, leaving death and desolation in their wake. The slaughtering savages kill the deer, bear, and buffalo. They take fish from the rivers and the sea. Scragg's murder, everything, even other Scragg. There is no other creature that kills their own like this, only the Scragg do it. They are an abomination.

We studied them from our sky vessels, watching the weeds grow and spread span after span, but our elders said they were no danger to us. We must leave them alone. Mwari has a plan for them. Some said the Scragg are good, like a forest fire. After the fire, the forest grows anew. It's good for the forest to refresh. Scragg are like a forest fire, a devouring conflagration.

It went on like this for thousands of spans. We tended the gardens, forests, and oceans and watched the Scragg destroy our work. The elders said, leave them to their mischief. The way they war against each other, soon there will be no Scragg, but their numbers grew.

When they weren't warring and murdering each other, they were breeding. They would breed their entire tribe, then steal women from warring tribes and breed them. Some said they breed constantly for the pleasure of it, disgusting as that sounds.

Their numbers increased. They hump and rut more often than rabbits and don't birth their young in spring like the birds and deer. They birth throughout the span. No matter how many of their kind they killed, the weed grew.

Despite the Scragg, our people prospered. We built grand cities with gleaming palaces, excelled at the sciences, and understood the intricacies of nature down to molecules, the atom and beyond. Everything we learn, we use for good purpose to improve our ability to work with nature because Mwari loves us, and we love Mwari. Our reward is her gratitude that showers us with blossoming flowers.

At some point long ago, a group of elders decided we should make our presence known to the Scragg. The elders sent small groups out, never to return. Our missionaries were fresh meat for the Scragg. Despite the tragedies, our leadership was determined to domesticate them. We thought we could tame them like dogs. It proved not so different, but more difficult.

Prophecy foretold that when we give Scragg the gift of knowledge, they will value the garden. They will learn to live with nature instead of killing it.

We must give them a chance, the elders said. Mwari wants us to be kind to the Scragg, as we are with all the creatures in the garden. Karanga are avowed to a mission of husbandry, our elders said.

So we went. We travelled in great numbers on grand journeys bearing gifts and tools. In the beginning, the Scragg did not understand. Many karanga were killed, turned-on spits over Scragg fires. Although it took great strength and courage, by Mwari we did not kill them back. They must have thought us weak.

Some say we were the stupid ones going to the Scragg again and again. A Scragg's reaction when they see something new is to kill it and eat it, instead of learning from it.

After a time, the Scragg understood we did not come to war with them, and we discovered our technology astounded them. Our devices and sky vessels amazed them. They marveled at our metals that gleam in the sunlight. Some Scragg thought we were Mwari. We told them we were not. We explained we came to teach them to live in harmony with the garden. They thought us strange.

Over time, we taught them to make bread. We taught them to sow corn and rice. We taught them that the tubers growing in the dirt beneath their feet will nourish their bodies. There is no need to kill for meat.

They learned about corn and rice, but what the Scragg wanted were the shiny things, our metals that gleam in the light. To the Scragg, metal holds strength and power. The elders agreed we would not teach them, and we did not.

They stole it.

The Scragg steal everything, and it's our fault. After a time, we stopped visiting the Scragg. We had taught them enough. Some karanga said we taught them too much. We gave them a taste of what could be, what they can grow and what they can make. We became a vision of what they could become. They aspired to be us, even though they can never be like us. No matter what the Scragg have achieved, they are stupid.

The change of ages came when our garden spun through a massive frozen cloud. Many of our gardens, rivers, and oceans froze under thick ice. Karanga did our best to save every creature, but we lost many. The karanga cried to Mwari, but our tears turned to ice. Yet, even with most of the garden buried under deep glaciers, we achieved a tenuous balance.

The Scragg, who used to rove in small tribes throughout the garden, moved to southern regions where the garden still flourished. More Scragg in a smaller area pushed them into larger groups. Where had they all come from? More of them were in the garden than we'd ever seen. There was fierce fighting between warring tribes. Large armies formed to wage war for control of land and resources. Where there are Scragg, there is death. Some of our elders predicted this would be the end of the Scragg, but soon the fighting all but ceased.

Karanga had stopped visiting Scragg long ago. Most Scragg knew us only from stories told around campfires. Their young grew up listening to tales of the noble karanga who brought knowledge and skill to the Scragg.

Scragg love stories.

Some Scragg are smarter than the others. Maybe not smart. Devious is more accurate because they manipulate others for their benefit, like thieves. The devious ones stood before the mass of Scragg with painted faces wearing ridiculous costumes proclaiming to be the descendants of karanga. Their clumsy attempts at emulating our dignity and beauty were preposterous, but the grand performances captivated the Scragg.

The Scragg masses were told that karanga froze the garden because he was angry with the Scragg. They must bow before the descendants of karanga, for only they knew the sacred teachings. Scragg must follow the teachings and live like karanga to calm his anger. The Scragg listened and followed.

Scragg leaders who claimed themselves as descendants of karanga called themselves Munatsi, those who make us perfect. These Munatsi quickly gained power. They became priests and kings. We karanga watched, amazed that warring killers could transform into a population of builders. Working together, they built vast cities.

It dumbfounded us when they converted mountains to metal. We had not dared teach them for fear they would use metal for warring. After many spans, they started creating devices like ours. They built Yeshiri, vessels that fly like small birds. Their flying craft were not like the grand karanga ships, but the advancement of the Scragg continued to astound us. Our elders said the Scragg can only make what they have seen. They have no imagination. If they have seen something, it might take a thousand spans, but eventually their hands will learn to make what is in their mind.

Sheets of ice crippled the garden for over twenty thousand spans. No number of temples the Scragg built to honor karanga could relieve his anger. Even though the Scragg built amazing cities and many marvelous things to enhance the lives of their people, they still found time to war. Their technology brought larger wars with devastating weapons that killed more of their kind. Instead of petty battles between tribes over food and women, Scragg wars of that age were waged between great cities with powerful machinery and weapons, causing great destruction. In the temples they prayed to karanga to restore the garden, but in the jungles, they gorged on their unsated taste for blood.

While the Scragg warred and murdered, we karanga tended the gardens and oceans working to restore the world. After a time, the thick ice sheets began to recede. Birds flew north, carrying seeds. Trees grew in the thaw. Glaciers dripped water like honey, tumbling down the rocks into streams. Soon, great lakes held the waters back. We karanga joyously watched the plants blossom and gardens come to life again.

Then they came.

Somehow, they found our cities. The Scragg came by the thousands in sleek, fierce Yeshiri. Their flying birds, armed with fire and steel, destroyed our houses, and burned our buildings. They swarmed the karanga, killing all they saw.

I said earlier that karanga are warriors, but this was not our way before the Scragg attacked. All the times the Scragg killed karanga we did not kill them back, but when they filled the skies like clouds of locust leaving karanga dead in the streets, they left us no choice.

Most karanga had never seen a Scragg. They are ugly to our eyes and smell like death from meat rotting in their teeth. Karanga did not want to fight. We watched thousands die, our brothers and sisters' bodies lying at our feet.

The Scragg did not stop. We had done nothing to them, but they kept coming.

Their Munatsi prayed to us. They did all they could to be like us. The Scragg cried out to karanga to save them, yet they came to kill us. Did they know what they were killing?

Scragg kill because they can. It is their will, their nature. They do not ask or try to understand. It does not matter what they kill, only that they can kill it. If they kill all karanga, who will tend the garden?

We killed them back.

Now it was Karanga who learned from the Scragg. Karanga fashioned weapons. We designed new sky vessels, Dhiragoni that resemble dragon flies and sleek fighters, the Hondo Bhagi that spit fire. We trained every young male and female karanga as warriors. Karanga learned to fight and kill. We do not murder. Karanga only kill, to not be killed. We fight with honor for the survival of karanga and the gardens.

I felt a hand on my shoulder, turned and saw Raviro standing over me. "What are you doing, Mas?" Raviro is short, petite, and motherly. She may not look like a warrior, but she is strong, and her faith is solid as a rock. Without Raviro, we would have died long ago.

"Writing." I felt embarrassed and blanked my screen. "It helps pass the time."

Raviro was curious, but didn't press me. "Anything to report?"

"The water tank is low. There were no extra flows during these spans. Maybe Mwari has forgotten us."

"As long as karanga tend the gardens, rivers, and oceans, Mwari will watch over the karanga," Raviro said tenderly rubbing my shoulder.

"Maybe that's the problem. We aren't tending to the garden. We are lost, barely surviving. Karanga was losing the battle against the Scragg. What if we are the last karanga? What happens when there are no karanga to tend the garden?"

"Mas Gwinyai, don't you dare lose faith. Mwari will never forsake us. Do not worry, it causes you distress. You have done your duty and deserve to rest. Go to your pod. I will watch the limb and ask Mwari for extra water."

I shuffled to my pod and prepared to hibernate for the next five spans, with thoughts of war heavy on my mind.

Chapter Two

Five spans later.

The hike across the lava bed was strenuous. Wisps of dust marked the narrow trail over black rock, its sharp edges cut boot tread and scuffed leather. When the trail disappeared, a compass was their guide. The sun beat down on the porous rock, making the trek more arduous. The wide horizon made the ancient lava flow appear endless, stretching to the distant mountains.

Ten students from Dr. Dale Clark's graduate program trailed behind the tall, sturdy man dressed in khaki hiking pants, green plaid shirt, and a wide-brimmed hat. Mechanized carts loaded with equipment navigated slowly over the uneven terrain.

The trek took them deep into a no-man's-land of desolate landscape where nothing grows. A place where hope quickly fades if one loses their way.

Even the professor who had made this trek before was relieved when he spotted the object of their quest. As they approached their destination, the doctor and his students stood in awe observing the odd feature that was out of place and outside of time. The doctor was pleased to see his students struck with wonder and excitement.

Before them, a solitary spire of shimmering black obsidian rose eighteen feet out of the lava bed, standing alone against the barren landscape. The black glasslike rock glinted in the sunlight. The lava around the base of the spire was smoother, worn from a thousand footsteps made by curious visitors over the millennia.

"Stop for a moment to admire its majesty, because what you see should not exist. Not here. Not anywhere, because there is nothing else like it. This lonely obsidian monolith you stand before defies science and geology. Can anyone tell me how this object formed?"

A young man in his twenties with a scruffy beard answered. "It's not a postpile. Those are long columns of hexagonal lava that cool slowly in long vertical fractures. Besides, postpiles don't form as solitary spires. We find them in large formations."

The professor smiled with approval. "Good Bruce, anyone else?"

Larry, a thin young man with shaggy blond hair, was quick to add more. "The lava flow we've been hiking over the past two hours is basalt. A wide, slow-moving river of magma formed this lava bed. The mineral composition of basalt is all wrong for obsidian."

Rohan, a short Pakistani boy wearing black-rimmed glasses, spoke quickly to ensure he was included in the discussion. "Basalt is rich in iron and magnesium composed mainly of olivine, pyroxene, and plagioclase."

"Good observation, Larry, and right out of the textbook, Rohan. It's clear the spire is not basalt. I asked how this obsidian spire could have formed here."

A young female raised her hand. "We aren't in the classroom, Emma. Speak up."

"Thank you, Doctor Clark. An obsidian spire surrounded by a basalt lava flow makes little sense. Like Larry said, the mineral composition is wrong. Obsidian is rich in silica formed by rapid cooling. Could there have been a vein of viscous lava that shot up under pressure through the flow?"

"Good question, Emma. The answer is, we don't know how it formed. That's the mystery of it. Let's step closer because the mystery gets stranger as this spire takes us on a journey from geology to archeology."

Doctor Clark walked to the glossy spire and rubbed his hand along the smooth object. "Studies prove that early man gathered at this location for many millennia. Ancient campsites and firepits are nearby. There is evidence of religious ceremonies, possibly even human sacrifice. We believe humans considered this location sacred for at least five thousand years, possibly much longer than that."

Rohan reached out and rubbed his hand along the cool, glassy surface. "You can feel the hieroglyphics inscribed on the spire."

Dr. Clark huffed. "Someone has been reading ahead. Don't spoil it for everyone, Rohan."

Rohan balked. "It's on Wikipedia. It's not like we're the first ones here."

"Well then, why doesn't Rohan tell us more?"

The thin young man pushed his glasses up his nose and stepped around the spire to examine the monolith. "The spire is cylindrical. It's six inches in diameter at the top and broadens to eight inches at ground level. It has three sets of identical markings at different points along its length. The markings are not Egyptian, Hindi, or Mayan and don't match any native American art. They are utterly unique and totally indecipherable. Scientists cannot agree on how the markings were etched in the material. Obsidian, as we know it, is brittle. It's easy to chip, not much stronger than window glass, but this material is harder than diamonds. Ancient man did not have the tools to carve these markings. This is not your typical obsidian spire, by any standard."

Charlie, a stout young man with a mustache, scoffed. "As if there are any typical obsidian spires."

Professor Clark placed a hand on the spire, feeling the cool, glassy surface. "Very good. Rohan has proved the power of the written word. We are not the first people here, not by a long shot. We are here to take a step further, to go where no man has gone before. A ground penetrating radar survey completed last year discovered a void below the spire that begins just three feet beneath the layer of lava. We are here to learn if this void is simply a large scoria which you all know is a volcanic bubble created by dissolved gas as the lava cooled, a mysterious vortex, an oddity in soil composition, or the ancient tomb of a long-dead king. We'll set up camp in the clearing at the edge of the lava flow. Our work of adventure and discovery begins tomorrow."

Professor Clark was pleased with himself; his students were excited and energized. Maybe he'd been overly dramatic. After all, his students knew why they were there. Still, he didn't want them to take the significance of the spire for granted. The spire was old. Did ancient man create the spire to mark the mysterious void below? Previous excavations of the surface layer had turned up some artifacts, but nothing of significance. The project his students embarked upon would delve to break through the lava flow, and dig below the surface, attempting to reach the void, solve the mystery of the spire and learn what lay below. If they were going to dig it up, they should at least have some respect for it.

The next morning, the students marked off a thirty-by-thirty-foot area with pegs and twine to outline the excavation site. They then drilled a series of holes in a grid pattern through two feet of lava at eighteen-inch intervals around the spire. One by one, they dropped explosives into the holes and snaked wires from each hole across the ground to a black box set a safe distance from the excavation site.

Charlie called out. "Clear the area."

"Stand back," Bruce added.

The students huddled around Doctor Clark. "Emma, would you like the honor?" he asked, presenting a handheld detonator to her.

Emma smiled. "It would be my pleasure." She looked at her classmates. "Ready to make history, guys?"

She lifted the red switch cover, and with a flick of her thumb, flipped the toggle.

The blast lifted the rock bed a foot in the air in a rapid series of loud pops, then rumbled, shaking the ground as the broken rock fell in a cloud of dust.

Larry shouted with glee, "We have lift-off!"

Emma shrieked. "It happened so fast. I didn't know what to expect."

Dr. Clark stood, brushing dirt from his khaki slacks. "Alright team, now for the heavy lifting. Move the rocks to the designated area so we can clear the site."

By noon the next day, the chunks of blasted lava were hauled away, and two feet of red clay removed. The students worked hard, sweating under the scorching sun, digging the hard red dirt with large shovels. Charlie was the first to call out when his shovel struck a hard surface. "Doctor Clark. I hit something."

Then Rohan's shovel pinged like it hit steel. He brushed the dirt away with his hand. "Wow. Come look." Everyone in the group ran across the dig to see what Rohan had found. "More obsidian," he said, pushing dirt away to expose the glistening black rock.

Out came the brushes and small spades. The team worked on their hands and knees, clearing the surface of the void.

Chapter Three

I woke as my pod cover slid back. It begins again, the mind-numbing repetition of another five-span shift. Sometimes I wish we could have died in battle, like so many of our brave karanga. We would have died with honor instead of, ugh, the dammed umbilical tube. That's one feeling I'll never get used to, it's as if I touched a nerve that twinges deep in my spine. I take a quick roll in the hot sand to clean up, climb to the flight deck, and grab a handful of chika. They feel slimy. My hand is full of deformed, rotten grubs. I don't mind the rotten ones; they have more flavor, but the mangled, deformed ones set my anger a fire. I check the growing bins, they're nearly empty.

"Banga, you lazy gink. The chika are almost gone and half of them are rotten."

Banga sat in the pilot's seat staring at the broad forward display, viewing the replay of a battle fought long ago.

He was unmoved, his eyes locked on the screen, his hands gripping the flight controls. My anger swelled. "You're going to starve us. Watching battle replays for a thousand spans won't keep us alive."

Banga turned in his seat, snarling, which meant he was ready to fight. "We've inbred the mongrels too many times. They're dying out and we'll be next. You've got five spans. See if you can do better." Banga is taller than most karanga. His broad shoulders and hulking arms complete the image of the ideal karanga warrior. His brutish disposition matches his looks.

The battle replay caught my attention. I knew it well, but the scene pulled me in. Banga was viewing the most important battle of our lifetime.

"Scragg cutter on our tail," Raviro shouted from her pedestal behind and to the right of Banga in the pilot's seat.

Banga shouted orders. "Hang on. I'll do a forward loop and come up behind them. Mas, prepare to fire." Banga pushed the flight control forward.

I watched a battle I had lived through long ago. I know how it ends. It could have been Banga's excitement, but the scene mesmerized me. I stepped to my pedestal on his left and felt the familiar grip of the kumutsa lock my feet in place.

Our vessel, a Hondo Bhagi, or battle bug, flies faster than the large karanga Dhiragoni dragon fly ships. Our small ship is shaped like an almond and, like that small seed, our bugs have protective armor. The black metallic shell encasing our ship does not have windows. Eyes embedded in the hull project what they see on the interior walls of the bug. Flying in a Hondo Bhagi is a glorious experience. You fly through the open sky as if no ship exists and gaze at the blue sky and clouds around you. Look down to view expansive gardens and the ocean below. Flying a bug feels like you're in a dream soaring through the open sky, but don't be fooled. We did not build the Hondo Bhagi for our pleasure. We designed them to stop the Scragg. Our bug is well-equipped to spit fire and launch chombo, explosive projectiles.

Our fleet of bugs led many battles against the notorious Scragg Cutters. Cutters are larger and more advanced than the old Scragg Yeshiri, but smaller than the enormous high altitude Scragg Cruisers. Their Cutters are fearsome because they pack two huge canons in their bow that deliver a massive destructive force. The Scragg Cutters proved devastatingly effective against karanga city defenses, destroying city walls, and collapsing our beautiful palaces. Only the speedy, hard-shelled Hondo Bhagi can get close enough to disable a Cutter.

Banga shouted again. "We're coming around. Get him locked in your sights."

I aimed my targeting system at the large vessel. "Closer, closer, got him. Target locked. Firing. Chombo, chombo, chombo."

Three missiles were on their way. We watched as the sonic speed projectiles raced through the sky, hitting the Cutter's engines in a fiery explosion. We cheered. I remember Raviro's excitement and Banga's look of triumph.

Our karanga pride was short-lived.

Raviro dampened our spirits, gasping. "Oh dear, Mwari, help us." As Banga turned our bug away from the explosion, we spotted six Scragg cutters and a cruiser on our right.

Banga's voice cracked. "They're heading for the northern lake."

Fear seemed to suck all the oxygen from our flight deck, but I knew we must act with resolve. I turned to Raviro. "Signal all the Hondo Bhagi. By Mwari, we must stop them."

The gardens had warmed. The retreating ice exposed new lands. As the glaciers melted, vast lakes formed in the north, covering extensive areas. Tenuous dams, earthen walls of ice and mud held the waters back.

We karanga worked to direct the lake waters to the oceans, but war with the Scragg kept karanga from our duties. Karanga were dying in vast numbers, leaving few of us to tend the gardens. The Scragg took advantage of our weakness and implemented a new horrific tactic.

The Cutters used their gigantic cannons to blast the massive walls of ice and mud, sending torrents of raging water down to flood cities and gardens. Massive floods wiped out karanga and the Scragg alike. Scragg don't care who dies. Scragg's fight to win, no matter the cost.

A dozen Hondo Bhagi joined us to face off the advancing Scragg fleet.

Banga scanned the sky. "Where's everyone else?"

Raviro checked her monitors. "There is no one else."

I stared at a sky filled with Scragg vessels and pushed away the fearful thoughts that crept into my mind. A dozen bugs, no matter how fast we flew or how well we shot, can't destroy a sky full of cutters and cruisers, but a warrior must not let fear stop him.

I swallowed hard. "The rest of our fleet is fighting over the eastern gardens. If we're going to stop these Scragg, it's up to us." I hoped I sounded brave.

Raviro radioed the other bugs. "Form up. Prepare to attack."

Banga accelerated, propelling our bug into the path of the Scragg Cutters. "Blitz them with everything we've got. Aim for their big guns."

When the shadow of a cutter blocked the sky, I failed to hold my feelings in check. "It's suicide, Banga. A dozen bugs against six Cutters and a cruiser, they'll wipe us out."

With fiery eyes, Raviro warned me, "Think of the people down there. If we don't stop the Scragg now, they will sweep away the last of the western cities."

Banga flew our craft at great speed toward the oncoming fleet. "No more talking. Now we fight."

"Now we die," I muttered.

Raviro held her gaze at me. "May Mwari be with us."

Banga growled over the open channel to our fleet of bugs. "Spread out, fly fast, and target well."

Our Hondo Bhagi zipped across the sky at low altitude, holding back our weapons until we got close to the Cutters.

They saw us coming.

Scragg fighters poured out of the high-altitude cruiser, outnumbering our bugs three to one.

Our speedy, agile bugs charged at the fighters, spitting fire. The fighters fired back. The Cutters and Cruiser above us dropped flak, altitude detonating ordinance, filling the sky with explosions and smoke.

Banga held steadfast navigating with spins and rolls, swerving past exploding flak and dodging missiles while hot lead pinged off our hard shell. We bounced past mid-air explosions, knowing a direct hit would be the end of us. Somehow, through it all, Banga kept us on course with the cutter we targeted.

The other bugs were struggling. In my headset I heard panicked voices, cries of desperation and the last words of our fellow karanga pilots as they went down one by one.

"They're all over us. We're taking heavy fire."

"We're hit, going down."

"Goodbye fellow warriors."

While our bugs were being crushed under the unrelenting assault of the Scragg fighters, one courageous voice broke through, lifting our spirits.

"We will make it. I have target lock."

Raviro cheered. "That's Vimbo. He's going to fire." We watched Vimbo's bug shoot up through the sky toward a cutter. Vimbo's bug fired its missiles at the Cutters' monstrous cannons, with Scragg fighters hot on his tail.

We tracked Vimbo's missiles arcing through the sky as they closed on the cutter. Seconds before impact, the missiles exploded, stopped by Scragg rockets.

Vimbo cried out. "We are the final missile. Chombo, chombo, chombo." His vessel slammed into the underbelly of the cutter, causing an enormous explosion. The cutter sent a volley of cannon fire at the massive dam as the belly of the large vessel erupted. We watched explosions rip through the airship's hull as the massive cutter broke up and fell from the sky.

Raviro and I cheered Vimbo's victory and the cutter's demise, but our enthusiasm vanished as we watched the fleet of Cutters, now in range, fire their cannons at the ice wall. With each pounding blast, the earthen dam weakened.

Raviro gasped. "Oh no! The dam's about to rupture."

Banga turned our bug in a sudden evasive move. "We've got Scragg fighters to worry about."

I fired our rear guns, spitting an endless stream of hot metal. "Two of them on our tail."

Flak exploded all around us, sending concussive shocks through our bug. Banga steered erratically, banking hard to the left, then hard to the right through exploding flak.

Raviro gripped her monitor to avoid being tossed around. "Are you crazy, Banga? You're flying directly at the ordinance."

I cursed under my breath. "He's going to kill us."

Banga edged his way to fly just above the detonation altitude of the flak. The vicious bombs were exploding behind and below us. The fighters were closing the gap. Our spitting metal had little effect on them. The fighters were nearly on us.

Alarms sounded from my pedestal. I shouted with fear. "Scragg have target lock."

Their rockets would fire in a matter of seconds. I looked at Raviro. She looked into my eyes, knowing the end was near.

Then it happened. The fighters disintegrated in violent flashes of fire, destroyed by their own Scragg flak.

Banga snarled. "Ha! Stupid Scragg." Banga pushed our craft faster, leaving the falling wreckage behind.

We were now flying above the dam. Scragg Cutters converged on our right, pummeling the wall with their cannon fire. The vast ocean of water that stretched before us captivated me. That view of the golden sun reflecting off the peaceful ripples was a sight I shall never forget.

Taking in the beauty, I whispered. "What a glorious sight."

Raviro caught me gazing at the water below. "Oh, how I long for this war to end so we can return to the gardens."

Banga, proud of his victory over the Scragg fighters roared with excitement. "That day is soon Raviro."

A metallic glint at the edge of the sun caught my eye. "What is that?"

Before we knew it, he was on us. A fighter blocked by the glaring sun flew directly at us. Hot lead bounced off our bug, ringing like a bell. Banga rolled to the left and pushed our bug into a steep dive, skimming the dam wall. I fired our rear guns, forcing the fighter to keep his distance.

Our Hondo Bhagi raced down the face of the steep dam, as the wall of ice and mud crumbled, breaking apart. The cannons of the Scragg Cutter's had accomplished their goal.

Banga pulled out of the dive, steering away from the crumbling dam as a two-hundred-foot wall of water burst through the collapsing mud. The torrent of water engulfed the Scragg fighter, crushing it under the weight of the giant wave.

Banga pushed our little bug as fast as it would fly, hoping to outrun the raging, angry waters roiling and churning behind us, but the deluge swept over us, sending our ship tumbling like a seed bobbing through the rapids.

Our small vessel bucked and rolled in the turbulent water. Banga cursed the controls. Our engine was dead. We had seen the widespread destruction caused by floods in the East. Massive walls of water swept over entire continents, wiping away any trace of karanga and Scragg cities alike, drowning every creature in the deep swirling water. The flood instantly erased civilizations and the glorious gardens that were built over thousands of spans, leaving death in its wake. There was nothing we could do but ride out the flood and hope for the best.

Banga stopped the playback, cursing himself for the ten thousandth time, thinking of everything he could have done differently. He blames himself, but I have no blame for him. I know he did his best. We are not dead.

Banga, obsessed with his defeat, started the playback again. But my mind focused on the events that followed.

Our bug floated with the swift muddy waters, hitting broken walls, and bumping over rocks. The water grew murky, blocking our ship's eyes. Our interior walls went dark, blinding us, making the experience more terrifying. We discussed escaping, but opening the hatch would flood the vessel, sinking it quickly. Karanga are not good swimmers. We agreed to ride with the current.

I remember Banga turning in his seat to face us with a defeated look. "I switched on the beacon. Karanga will find us."

After a time, our Hondo Bhagi stopped with a thump. We were upright, which was a blessing.

We were blind to what awaited us outside. Were we under water or stuck in debris? It was Raviro's idea to extend the limb at the rear of the ship. The limb is a tube designed to dock our bug with Dhiragoni. We carried spare eyes, but they are too large for the limb. We agreed. If we extended the limb and water poured in, we would pull it back before the ship flooded.

Cautiously we sent the limb up. No water. Our bug filled with fresh air and with it a breath of hope. Banga pressed the switch to open the hatch, but it didn't budge. The hatch mechanism struggled and whined. The door would not open. We tried for hours to force it. Nothing worked. We were trapped.

Feeling despondent, I turned away from Banga and his battle video. Being reminded of our endless predicament would not help me live out the next five spans.

Boom! A loud blast rocked our bug violently, throwing me to the floor. Banga braced himself, then leapt from his seat. "We're being attacked."

The blast deafened me. "I'll wake Raviro," I shouted, stumbling to the lower deck.

Our boredom had been disturbed only one other time, thousands of spans before, when our bug filled with choking smoke and acrid odors. We tried to retract the limb, but it wouldn't budge, so we sealed the end to stop the fumes from suffocating us.

When our vessel grew unbearably hot, we retreated to our pods for protection from the heat. Without the stable environment of our pods, we would have roasted to death.

Banga woke after two spans. The heat had diminished. He woke us. We unsealed the limb and our vessel filled with fresh air. Since that time, our only excitement are the rare days when an excess of water drips from the limb into the bucket.

Raviro joined us on the flight deck. "What do you think it was?"

I paused, straining my ears, expecting another shock, but no further blasts came. "Maybe It was an earthquake."

Banga dropped back into his pilot's seat. "That was no earthquake. The blast came from above."

Raviro's composure changed from fearful to hopeful. "Karanga have found our beacon. They're searching for us."

Her faith was encouraging. Why does Banga always think the worst? "Could it be? Karanga have come to rescue us, after all this time?"

Banga marched to the armory. "You'd better hope it's karanga." He returned, laying three handguns and a lightning lance on a table.

Raviro was aghast. "What are you doing?"

Banga picked up his lance, then gripped the handle, sending a buzzing arc of blue lightning to the tip of the spear. "I'm getting prepared. We're at war, don't you remember?"

I took a cautious step back. "You believe the war continues?"

Banga set down his lance, then started breaking down an ELF handgun for inspection. "Don't know if it does. Don't know that it doesn't. A warrior prepares. We must be ready to defend ourselves."

We did not question Banga. None of us knew what caused the violent shock. Would there be another blast? Were karanga searching for us, or was it something, or someone else? All we could do was wait. We were used to waiting, so we sat together cleaning, oiling, and charging our weapons. And we listened. We listened for hours and heard nothing.

Raviro broke the silence. "It could have been an earthquake."

Banga snarled with indignation. "You were asleep. How could you know?"

Then we heard it. Clink! The sound of metal striking metal. The sound woke every cell in my body, heightening my senses. "It came from above."

Banga grunted in agreement. "Just like the explosion."

Clink. We heard the sound again, followed by faint rumbling across the roof of our vessel.

Chapter Four

Exposed and swept clean, the surface of the void lay bare. What they had uncovered surprised Dr. Clark and his students. This void wasn't an anomaly caused by changes in soil composition or a hollow bubble in the volcanic rock, but a solid almond-shaped object made entirely of obsidian, with the spire near the end of the black rock that narrowed in width. Dr. Clark examined the smooth sloping mirror-like surface.

"It's amazing. I've never seen anything like it. The entire surface is a solid piece of obsidian. There isn't a groove, cut, or fracture anywhere on the entire object."

Larry, the tall blond student, moved from point to point along the surface, taking photos of the glossy black object with his phone. "I bet it's extraterrestrial. An alien probe sent a million years ago to study Earth."

The professor smirked. "As scientists, we must avoid making wild assumptions, Larry. Please reserve your conclusions until we have fully studied the object." The professor stood in thought for a moment. "We're going to need a massive crane and a flatbed trailer to move this to the university."

Bruce ran across the sloping surface. "Dr. Clark, Charlie says there's something you need to see."

Dr. Clark followed Bruce, stepping across the rock to the far side of the void. He stood, looking over his hot, dirty students, who were digging a wide trench that encircled the void. "What is it, Charlie?"

Charlie used a cloth to wipe the red dirt from the lower part of the exposed rock. "We found a seam that starts about six feet down, just above the point where the rock undercuts."

Dr. Clark climbed down a ten-foot ladder to get a closer look. "You have good eyes, Charlie. This seam, as you call it, looks like a hairline fracture. The light needs to be just right to see it." Dr. Clark rubbed his hand across the shiny, smooth rock. "I can barely feel it."

Charlie ran his finger along the seam. "At first, I thought it was a fracture or imperfection in the rock, but look at the shape. It runs horizontal for three feet, then curves straight down on both sides."

Rohan was on his knees, digging fiercely to expose more of the seam. "Hey, I see something." He brushed the dirt away, then used the flashlight on his phone to examine the area. "There are four faint squares, each with an etching inside. Each has a character like the ones on the spire, but these are different." Rohan touched each of the squares, then looked up at Dr. Clark. "This is a doorway, and those etchings are our way in."

The professor stood with a look of pride. "A doorway leading into the void. Will we discover the tomb of a long-lost king? Imagine the treasure that lies within. This is a monumental find. We're making history. This discovery will be my legacy. Good work everyone. Keep going, we're almost there."

Dr. Clark put his arm over Charlie's shoulder and pulled the young man close. "Excellent work, Charlie."

Dr. Clark moved to the ladder and began climbing. Rohan chased after him. "But the etchings I found, they're the key to understanding everything."

The professor stared down at the anxious young man, then scolded Rohan. "The etchings only help if we can decipher them. Until you can figure that out, make yourself useful with a shovel like everyone else." Rohan looked dejected, his face and knees covered with dirt.

When Dr. Clark reached the top of the ladder, he looked up at Bruce. "How soon until we have this masterpiece fully excavated?"

Bruce reached out to help his professor take the big step from the ladder to the slick sloping surface of the obsidian rock. "We've broken through the layers of thick clay, so the dirt is softer now. The way this obsidian structure is undercutting, we'll have the entire void dug out in a couple of hours."

We sat at the table long after we'd finished cleaning our weapons. Banga and Raviro sat, listening to the strange sounds, but I couldn't sit still, so I went to the lower deck to investigate.

When I came back, Raviro broke her long silence. "Did you learn anything? I wonder what's going on out there?"

Banga was losing patience. "The endless thumping and banging is giving me a headache."

"I heard entry error tones. I think someone was trying to open the hatch."

Banga's lips curled. "Then whatever it is, they are not karanga."

Raviro nodded agreement. "Banga's right. Karanga would know how to open the hatch."

"I also heard clinking and scraping all around the lower deck. It sounded like digging."

Raviro turned her head in thought. "Have we been buried all this time?"

I reached out and pressed my hand against the cold black wall. "I have often considered that possibility. It would explain why we have no eyes and why the hatch won't open."

Banga leapt to his feet. "If something is trying to reach us, we must prepare. We must go below and adorn ourselves in battledress."

Raviro raised her hand in caution. "We don't know what it is. It's best we don't appear combative. Aggression breeds mistrust and fear."

Banga pounded the table with his fist. "I will not exit this vessel without weapons."

I turned from the black wall looking at Banga, then Raviro. "You are both righteous. We are karanga and will conduct ourselves as karanga. We will not wear armor, but we will carry weapons for protection against the unknown. I have lived too many spans to die a hasty death."

The mechanized carts the students had used to carry gear were now covered with red clay and dirt from hauling loads of diggings up a dirt ramp from the deep trench to ground level. The students followed the carts as they headed to camp for their lunch break.

Rohan stayed behind, digging at the front of the smooth black rock, clearing away the last layers of dirt from its underside. He carefully brushed the surface, searching for more etchings. If he could find another etching, he might discover the key to decode the strange glyphs. As he wiped the smooth rock, he discovered an area with greater translucence, allowing him to peer deeper into the black, glassy object. He examined the area, trying to peer inside.

Black lids separated, exposing a large white eyeball with a brown iris and black pupil. The eye shifted left and right, then blinked, fixing its gaze on him.

Rohan shrieked with fright, falling backward in the dirt. He stared into the eye that seemed to examine him. Its iris rotated and the pupil dilated. Rohan scrambled to his feet and screamed, running up the ramp, "It's alive! It's alive. I saw it."

Rohan ran to a group of students gathered at Dr. Clark's tent. "It has eyes. It looked at me. There's something inside the void."

Dr. Clark, Bruce, and Charlie accompanied Rohan to the front of the obsidian rock. Rohan dropped to his knees, rubbing the black glass, searching for the spot where he saw the eye, but he found nothing.

Rohan slapped his hand against the object in frustration. "There was a big eyeball right here. It stared at me. I'm telling you; this thing is alive."

Dr. Clark helped Rohan to his feet. "Take a break, son. You're trying too hard. Go to camp. Eat something and get some rest."

"I don't need rest. I know what I saw. There's something alive inside."

"Bruce, break out the weapons just in case. We need to prepare for whatever we find behind that door."

Charlie jerked his head toward the rectangular seam they'd discovered. "Any ideas on how we can get that door open?"

Dr. Clark shrugged. "I'm working on that. I've sent photos of the door and the etchings to colleagues at other universities, hoping someone can provide guidance."

"If all else fails, we've got more explosives," Bruce offered.

Charlie shook his head. "We can't risk using explosives. Besides, I doubt if that would work."

Dr. Clark smiled at Charlie. "Charlie's right. No explosives. We're smart people; we'll figure it out. In the meantime, let's get Rohan to camp."

Chapter Five

Raviro wore a colorful siketi wrapped around her waist that fell just above her feet, covered with a brilliant blue and green robe flowing from her shoulders. Her headdress, a simple korona of golden leaves.

I wore a man's brown siketi dyed in a pattern of ochre squares. A man's siketi is much shorter than what females wear. I also adorned myself with a majestic green and gold breast covering. Unfortunately, my korona had grown brittle and broke long ago, so I wore no headdress.

Banga mumbled and grunted behind his locker door until he timidly appeared, wearing a long red robe covered with a teal breast plate in the shape of an elm leaf and a helmet of acorn wood topped with deer antlers.

Raviro gave him a disapproving look. "I thought we were not wearing armor."

Banga grumbled. "After all these spans, I have nothing else that fits."

I laughed. "You have grown thicker, Banga."

Banga huffed and pointed at me. "The spans haven't been kind to you either, Mas Gwinyai."

Raviro stepped between us, extending her arms out gracefully. "We are karanga. We are beautiful and radiant. There is none who would look upon us and not bow with humility."

Raviro looked at the weapons arrayed on the table. Banga handed me a pistol. "Conceal your weapons. I shall carry the lance."

Checking myself, I asked. "Are we ready?"

Banga grunted. "I was ready ten thousand spans ago."

Raviro looked melancholy. "My heart aches to walk through the garden once again."

Banga stood at the hatch. Raviro and I stood nervously behind him, hoping we would soon escape the vessel that held us captured for endless spans. Banga placed his hand against the wall, then moved his fingers in a sequence the emitted joyful tones.

The door seal retracted with a loud pop. The hatch made a grating sound as it slid open, then a long black glass ramp extended to the ground.

Daylight blinded us. How long had it been since we saw sunlight? As our eyes adapted, we stared at a wall of red dirt. There was no sound. The pounding clamor had ceased. The three of us looked up at the brilliant blue sky. I sucked in the warm, thick air in deep breaths, reveling in the sun's warmth. It felt glorious to be outside.

Raviro studied the trench as we stepped forward. "Whatever dug this pit is gone."

Banga pointed his lance at the dirt ramp at the end of the trench. "Don't be quick to judge. Advance with care."

We gazed in shock as we reached the top of the ramp. The garden was dry and barren, covered with black lava rock. Ugly dead colors of black and brown were all I could see. I looked at Raviro. A tear streamed down her cheek. A deep pain seared in my heart. Our garden was dead.

We stepped along a dirt path leading across the jagged lava. I heard awful squawking sounds in the distance that reminded me of an injured bird. Banga spun to face the terrifying sounds.

He raised his lance in a defensive posture and shouted, "Scragg!"

Raviro and I stood frozen, shocked by the sight of the ugly creatures, my ears pained by their screeching voices.

The students stood in a line holding bowls, waiting for Emma to serve them lunch. One by one, she filled each bowl with a heaping ladle of campfire stew.

Rohan sat alone on a rock, away from the others.

Emma smiled at Bruce as he held his bowl out to her. He looked into her eyes and smiled back. He lingered for a moment, but when he moved away, something in the distance caught Emma's attention. She stared at the excavation site, unsure of what she was seeing. Charlie was next, waiting. He tapped his bowl against the stew pot, but Emma didn't respond.

"Hey, I'm next. I hope you didn't give my portion to Bruce. Emma?"

Charlie turned to see what Emma was staring at.

He was stunned by what he saw, but called out. "Dr. Clark. We have visitors."

The professor turned and stared, awed by the strange creatures. The other students set down their bowls and looked in amazement.

Charlie pointed. "The one in front made a strange sound."

Dr. Clark held his gaze, observing the odd beings. "It looks like the tall one might attack. Bruce, Charlie, get the weapons."

I scanned the group of Scraggs. "They look stupid standing there, staring at us."

Raviro looked disgusted. "Why are they so ugly?"

I turned to Banga. "Are you certain they are Scragg? I've never seen one up close."

Raviro stepped to Banga's side. "Yes, Banga, are you sure? The images I've seen of Scragg are fleshy, bare chested creatures with long hair wearing siketi of animal skin or leaves."

Banga pointed his lance at the creatures. "They may have cut their hair and changed their dress, but they are Scragg. Don't approach. They are dangerous savages."

The sight of the Scragg made my skin crawl. "No matter how they adorn themselves, they are ugly."

Raviro sniffed the air. "They smell like rotting flesh. I think I may be sick."

I watched as the creatures gathered like a herd of cows chewing grass. "They don't look threatening."

Banga stuck the hilt of his spear in the ground. "Beware. They may look calm, but they can attack at any moment."

Emma dropped her ladle into the stew. "What kind of creature are they?"

Larry, the tall student with shaggy blond hair, edged close to her. "Maybe they're aliens, and we just dug up their spaceship."

Emma scoffed. "It's not a spaceship." Emma looked at Dr. Clark. "It isn't a spaceship, is it?"

The strange beings fascinated Dr. Clark. "I don't know. I think they're talking, but I can't make out any words. It's an unusual dialect, composed of guttural grunts and clicks."

Bruce and Charlie returned with pistols and handed a rifle to Dr. Clark.

Bruce looked at the creatures. "What are they?"

Charlie holstered his pistol and observed the beings for a moment. "Look at their long thin limbs, elongated skulls, their bulbous eyes, and narrow mouths. They resemble ants."

Emma quipped. "Ant people."

Dr. Clark dredged up some trivia he'd read somewhere. "The Hopi Indians told stories about ant people that helped them during times of great turmoil. Maybe they're friendly."

Emma studied what the creatures were wearing. "One looks female. I like her outfit."

Rohan pushed through the other students to get a look at the beings that had emerged from the void. "See, I told you there was something alive in there. I told you. You said I needed rest, but I was right. You never give me credit. I was right. I'm always right," Rohan stammered as he began walking steadfastly toward the ant people.

Emma cried. "Rohan stop. You'll scare them."

"It's OK. They've already seen me." Rohan broke into a run.

Dr. Clark called out. "Stop Rohan."

Rohan shouted as he ran. "They know me. They'll teach me. I want them to tell me everything."

A Scragg started running toward us. "Why is that one screeching?"

Raviro stepped behind Banga. "Is that it's war cry?"

"I told you they're Scragg. It's attacking." Banga responded by advancing like a warrior singing a karangan war song meant to scare humble creatures into submission. The Scragg did not stop. Banga marched, aiming the sharp lightning lance at the crazed Scragg.

The shrieking Scragg ran toward Banga. Banga trotted forward extending his lance, shouting his song. As the two creatures met, coming close, the needle like tip of the lance pierced the chest of the angry Scragg, running him through. The Scragg's body jerked, then slid down the metal spear, its body jolting with each pulse of blue lightning.

Panic spang me to action. "Raviro, take cover behind the cart." She ran to a mud-laden cart. I ran to another cart and drew my weapon.

Banga lifted his lance high in the air, the limp Scragg body hanging from it. He shouted a sorrowful cry, then flung the body aside.

Emma cried out. "They killed Rohan."

Bruce fired a shot, hitting the killer ant man's breastplate. The creature stumbled back a few steps, then stood erect, pumping the lance above his head, making a horrific squawking sound.

Dr. Clark held out his arm to stop his students. "Hold your fire. Rohan rushed them. How would you expect them to react?"

Larry picked up the pot of stew and stepped toward the ant people, speaking in a soft, friendly tone. "I told you it was aliens. They've been trapped in that spaceship for centuries. They're probably hungry."

Larry crept toward the aliens. "Hi ant people. You've been in your spaceship for such a long time. You must be hungry. We're having lunch. Would you like to join us?"

Dr. Clark shouted. "Larry, get back here. It's not safe."

Larry looked back. "They're just scared. I'll show them we're friendly." Larry tread on the dirt path toward the ant people. "We can be friends, mister ant man.

I don't want to hurt you. Finding your ship was a big surprise. I bet you're surprised to see us, too. We dug your ship out of the dirt. That means we're friendly. Now you're free. I bet your friendly too. Rohan was crazy. We don't blame you for that."

Raviro examined Banga. "Are you injured?"

Banga pounded his lance against his chest. "Ha! The Scragg weapons spit soft metal. They cannot pierce karanga armor."

I poked my head out from behind the cart. "Take cover Banga."

"I will not cower before savages."

Raviro pointed at the Scragg advancing toward us. "What now? Another one approaches."

I watched the man. He appeared calm, but carried something in his hands. "What is that crazy Scragg doing?"

Raviro held her nose. "He's trying to drive us away with that stinking pail of rotten flesh."

Banga took a defensive posture. "It's a Scragg trick. They'll trick us, then kill us dead."

Raviro touched a finger to the dirt covered lava, then waved her hand in a broad circle over the barren ground. As her hand passed over the brown grit, it turned green, springing to life as a bed of soft green clover.

Raviro called out. "I will defeat the stench of rot and death with the garden of life." Raviro stood behind her cart, moving her hands in sweeping movements, sending the bed of clover and blossoming flowers across the dirt path to the young Scragg's feet.

The sudden green growth startled the young man. He dropped the pail of hot stew, spilling hot dead meat on the fresh clover.

Raviro screamed, feeling the clovers pain. She flung her arms in dynamic movements, causing roots to sprout from the ground curling around the young Scragg's feet. The Scragg looked back at his friends with panic in his eyes screeching like a wounded dog as the trunk and bark of a tree rose, twisting around his legs, rising around the Scragg, encapsulating his body in gnarled wood. Tangled vines swirled around his outstretched arms, growing into long, broad branches of a flowering olive tree.

Raviro stood proudly, admiring the majesty of her work.

Larry stopped screaming when a branch of sprouting leaves grew out of his mouth, but his frightened eyes were still alive.

Dr. Clark raised his rifle, aimed, and fired. The bullet struck Larry in the forehead.

Emma screamed. "You shot Larry."

"He was as good as dead, dear. I put the poor boy out of misery."

Charlie raised his pistol and shouted. "They turned him into a frigging tree." He aimed and fired at the tree making ant. The bullet hit the cart the female ant stood behind, causing the strange being to duck.

Bruce fired an angry shot at the warrior ant. His bullet sheared an antler off the ant man's helmet.

Dr. Clark cried out. "Stop shooting. Calm down. We obviously don't understand what we're dealing with."

Bruce had an alien in his sight. "They've killed two of us. You want to wait for them to turn us into an orchard?"

Charlie stepped forward, aiming his pistol at the creatures. "Bruce is right. We need to take them out. End this now."

I gasped. "They shot the boy?"

Banga thumped his chest. "It's the Scragg way. They kill their own kind."

Raviro howled. "They shot at me too."

I scoffed. "Maybe they don't appreciate the beauty of a Scragg being entwined in an olive tree."

Raviro looked exasperated. "He hurt my clover with his rotten meat. I'm sorry, I have little patience after being trapped in that bug for ten thousand spans."

Banga beat his breastplate once again with his lance. "They keep trying to kill me, but I still stand."

I smiled. Banga looked silly with a single antler on his head, but I knew the situation was deteriorating. We were in dire peril. Scraggs were shooting at us, and we'd killed two of them. Scragg are tenacious. They fight to win, no matter the cost to their own. I was worried how this might end. "We can go back to the ship. Maybe the engine will start. They dug us out, we can leave."

Banga wasn't about to turn tail and give up the fight. "The engine will take time to repair. If we go to the ship, we'll get trapped again. More Scragg will come. They won't stop until they've killed us dead."

Chapter Six

The students huddled around Dr. Clark as he laid out his plan to end the siege. "Aim to wound or subdue them. I want them alive if possible. Use twine to tie them up. It would be a pity if all we had were dead specimens to show for our effort. Spread out. Bruce, take two others with you to cover the left flank. Charlie, you take two more and move to the right. That will leave two with me to hold the center. If you don't have a gun, grab a shovel. When you're in position, watch for my signal, then open fire."

The students moved to their positions, preparing for their attack.

Banga pointed at the Scragg scrambling around their camp. "They're on the move. They're planning to kill us dead. If we want to get out of this alive, we must kill them back."

Raviro wept. "I'm sorry if I caused this. I lost my temper."

Banga sighed. "It's not your fault. Scragg only understands death. It would have ended this way no matter what we did. It is the Scragg way."

I had hoped for better, but I knew Banga spoke the truth. The Scragg will kill us. The only way we survive is to kill them back. I stood behind the cart, aiming my ELF pistol at a male Scragg. "It's us or them. We have no choice. It's time to act." I pulled the trigger.

There was no bang, bullet, or projectile. Scragg's like things that go boom. Karanga pistols are silent and humane.

The pistol, equipped with a laser sight, projects a focused beam of extremely low frequency electromagnetic radiation or ELF tuned to a specific resonance that short circuits the Scragg brain. Target the red dot on the subject's head for five seconds and the Scragg drops to the ground, dead. The Scragg feels no pain. They don't even know what's happening until the beam simply switches them off, so to speak.

I held the dot steady, aimed at the side of the male Scragg's head until he tumbled to the ground.

"Down you go," I heard Banga shout, dropping another Scragg.

What makes this challenging is that Scraggs don't know they are supposed to stand still.

Loud pops from Scragg weapons filled the air with metal. I ducked, then aimed for a gunman on the right, but he moved after he fired. I couldn't hold the beam on him. Even worse, he was shooting at me. Bullets hit the cart and the dirt around my feet. I aimed my beam at him again, and he stumbled forward. He looked disoriented. Maybe the beam had done some damage, but he was still alive. He shot at me again, then stopped to reload. My hands shook as I aimed the red dot at his skull. He fired a wild shot, then fell forward on his face.

Banga killed a Scragg on my left.

Raviro groaned. "How are you doing that? I'm no good at this."

Banga held his weapon steady on a male Scragg as it moved through their camp. The male who had shot Banga's antler off. The man dropped to the dirt. Banga shouted. "I've dropped three of them. Keep up, Mas, or you'll get us killed."

"I'm trying, but they keep moving." I looked up to see a Scragg running at me, swinging a shovel. If I hadn't ducked, he would've taken my head off. Before I knew it, I was lying on the ground with the male Scragg on top of me. His mouth moved, squealing strange words.

I struggled with the ugly Scragg. You'd be surprised. They're stronger than they look. I felt his warm, stinking breath on my face. His skin was smooth and fleshy. I could barely believe I was touching a Scragg.

His blue eyes blazed as he fought to hold me down. I had often wondered what it would be like to encounter a Scragg. I hoped to learn something about him, to find kindness, but his eyes flashed with anger. He and his friends freed us. Why dig us out only to kill us?

I braced myself as another Scragg ran toward us, shouting an evil curse, carrying a length of cord. The fat smelly being skidded to a stop and dropped to its knees next to me. He was smiling as he spat out more words. These ugly Scragg never stop their infernal gibbering.

I pushed and kicked, fighting to free myself, but the heavy Scragg wedged my arms under his knees and wrapped his hands around my neck, squeezing the breath out of me. Why do you kill me? I have no desire to kill you. I only kill to not be killed. You are Mwari's creature. I am karanga. You pray to us. In your temples, you ask for our forgiveness and our blessing. Why kill what you aspire to become?

Seconds later, the one holding the cord fell on his comrade. I looked over and saw Banga smirking. "Shoot the one on top of me, damn you!"

"Free yourself, Mas Gwinyai. You don't want to hear me boasting for the next thousand spans that I earned all the glory on this day."

The Scragg holding me down looked frightened. I shouted back at him. "Get off, or you'll end up like your friend. Get off me." The Scragg shifted his weight to push his friend aside, giving me the opportunity to free my arm and aim the silent beam under his chin. He saw the red dot and looked down at me with curious eyes.

He made squawking sounds and swatted at my weapon, pushing it away, but I brought it back, directing the beam between his eyes.

The hulking brute fell on me. I nearly suffocated under his dead weight. After a moment, I gained the strength to roll the Scragg off me and stood. Exhausted from the struggle, I looked down at the Scragg. I had touched his skin and smelled his breath. I was not proud of his death.

 Raviro left the protection of her cart to follow Banga. I scurried to walk beside Raviro, letting Banga take the lead. Two Scragg were still alive. One had a long gun. As we approached, he fired at Banga. One bullet struck his breastplate, and the next cracked his helmet. Banga stumbled, but we steadied him. He removed his broken helmet, dropping it to the ground.

The Scragg tried to fire again. He would have killed us if he could, but his gun did not spit metal. As we advanced, he tossed his weapon to the ground and stood with his hands over his head. A female Scragg was on her knees, weeping.

The male squawked at us nonstop. Was he angry, threatening us, or pleading for mercy? Sometimes I wish I spoke Scragg, so I'd understand what the odd sounds meant. I think he was their leader. It was this one we saw laying the plans for the Scragg attack.

Banga screamed, reciting a war cry filled with rage. He sent lightning arcing across the tip of the lance he extended before him. The Scragg approached, squawking like an angry black crow. This was the Scragg who sent the others to fire metal at us and swing shovels at our heads to kill us dead.

Banga stood fearless, growling at the menacing Scragg. It was still jabbering when Banga thrust the tip of the lance into the Scragg's eye. Its head shook, jittering like a bug from the lightning in the lance. Banga pushed the spike through the Scragg's skull. The man slumped forward, putting his weight on the spear. Banga flung the Scragg aside, sending the body rolling to the ground.

The female was on her knees, crying. Raviro stood before her. The Scragg female rose on her knees, lowered her head, and held her arms out as if they were branches. She looked up and made the same movement with her arms a second time, head down, spreading her arms out. Maybe she desired to be entwined in a tree like her friend.

Raviro raised her weapon with an outstretched arm, pointing the gun at the female's head. The Scragg woman wailed. Tears dripped over pleading words. Raviro didn't fire. The female cupped her hands together and looked to the sky, muttering words as if praying. Was she praying to us?

Raviro's hand shook.

Banga stepped forward with his pistol raised. "If you can't do it, I will."

I pushed his arm down. "She is Mwari's creature. She has no weapon."

Banga pressed the barrel of his pistol against the female's head. "They shot at us. They tried to kill me."

Raviro dropped her arm. "I won't do it. She's helpless."

I pushed Banga's pistol away. "Let her go."

Banga shouted. "Without my armor, I would be dead. They kill us, we kill them back."

I reached out and helped the woman stand. "We are better than Scragg."

The female stepped forward and wrapped her arms around Raviro.

Raviro recoiled from the embrace.

Banga raised his weapon. "She's attacking."

I held him back. "Stop Banga."

Raviro smiled. "She's warm and squishy." The woman wept, moaning a sorrowful cry.

Banga pulled the Scragg woman off Raviro and pushed her away. "Leave us. Go."

Raviro wiped away a tear that was not hers. "She made my face wet."

Banga walked behind the female, pushing her to move along the dirt path. When they had passed the ramp, Banga gave her a last push. The female walked on, across the dark, barren field of lava.

Banga ran down the ramp toward our ship, shouting back at us. "We must prepare. Once the Scragg is away, she will bring more."

Raviro and I watched the female step awkwardly over the uneven lava. The sun beat down, causing the black rock and the woman's image to shimmer in the distance. The female turned, waved her hand, then continued walking.

Raviro dropped her gaze, then stepped gingerly through the Scragg camp. I stood over the dead, wondering why this had happened. The Scragg labored diligently to dig our ship out of the deep red clay. We owe them our freedom, yet it was their aggressive behavior when we greeted them that caused their demise.

I don't know why they attacked, first one, then the next until all fought to kill us. Will there be a day when karanga and Scragg are at peace? The elders say Scragg will never change. Did we misunderstand their actions? Did they dig knowing they would free us? Were they friendly yet frightened by our presence? No matter their intent, in the end they are Scragg and death follows them wherever they go.

I tended to the bodies, gathering them in a row, covering them with broken lava. Piling rocks on bodies is the Scragg way of honoring their dead. I read that somewhere.

Banga worked on the engine. His loud cursing and pounding told me he was making progress.

Raviro roamed the lava field, caressing the ground, swaying her arms like a conductor, breathing life into the desert, transforming the barren landscape into a garden.

Soon, the whine of our bug's engine sprung to life. Banga called out to us from the dirt ramp. "Let's go. We must leave before more Scragg arrive."

As we lifted off the ground, I looked down at a vast pine forest where black jagged rock had been. Raviro was smiling.

I am Majaya Masimba Gwinyai. I am karanga. We are an ancient people.

The End

I hope you enjoyed this short tale. If you did, there's more to the story. Click the link to read more episodes of Obsidian on Amazon's Kindle Vella. OBSIDIAN | Kindle Vella (amazon.com)

Authors Notes

Obsidian is an intriguing and thought-provoking tale. It's a story that takes place in a time long ago and yesterday. It's a fantastical view of a world wiped away at the end of an ice age. A story of war and devastating floods clearing the way for modern civilization. A study of cultural bias and misunderstandings that cause endless strife.

Why do we war, kill, and fight?

Are the Scragg human and the karanga something more, something different, something lost or somewhere hidden? How do humans treat other humans? How do we react when we stumble upon something we don't understand? Do we stop and learn when presented with something extraordinary, or do we dissect and destroy it? Can we rise above and be more like them, or are we slaves to our nature?

The karanga character names and many of the words are based on the Shona language. Shona is a Bantu language of the Shona people of Zimbabwe and Karanga is a dialect. I like the sound and tone of the words. Using these words, my goal is to add depth through language as an aid in developing the characters as an ancient noble people.

ASTEROIDS—Bridge to Nowhere

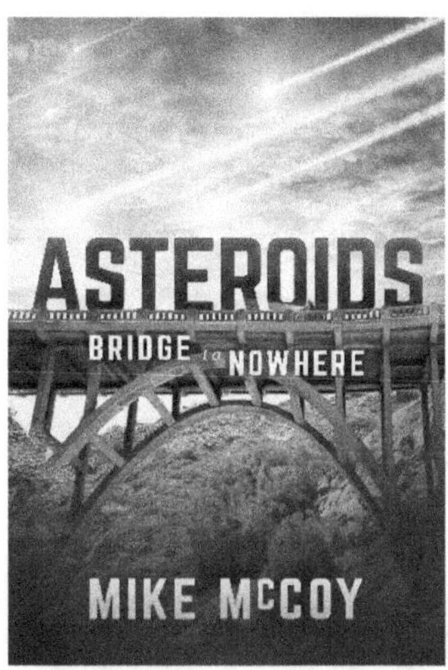

9.5 out of 10—The BookLife prize

Although asteroids hitting Earth is not a new story idea, McCoy brings a fresh approach to his apocalyptic plot. From the futuristic weapons to the artificial atmosphere of New Arcadia to the vampire-like antagonist who gains immortality from the blood of children, to two characters' use of Klingon as code, this story is full of unique ideas.

McCoy's combination of everyday language and scientific jargon is extremely well balanced. There isn't a boring passage in the book.

An asteroid storm of apocalyptic proportions is headed for Earth.

A mysterious group within the government called the Arcadian's led by Colonel Cruikshank knows the storm is coming. This corrupt shadow government has taken extreme measures to keep the storm secret while building underground cities to protect the *few and the fortunate*. Cruikshank's goal is that after the storm passes his survivors will emerge from the protected cities as a more perfect humanity. He is determined to create his Utopian society, no matter what it takes.

Rick Munday is a husband, father, and struggling Astrophysicist who needs his research grant approved. When Cruikshank learns that Rick's grant proposal predicts the asteroid storm, Cruikshank drugs and kidnaps Rick, securing him in the underground city of New Arcadia.

On his quest to escape the Arcadian's and reach his family, Rick, and friends he meets on his journey use high-tech hacking skills to warn the world of the coming disaster, expose the underground cities, and save thousands more souls. Captain Kobalt, Cruikshank's enforcer chases Rick and his friends across America in an epic adventure leading to a climactic conflict between Rick and Kobalt.

Asteroids—Bridge to Nowhere is a fast-paced near-future dystopian adventure. Watch out! Tribulation will get you out there….

You can also read the award-winning Coming-of-Age Story, On the Waterfront.

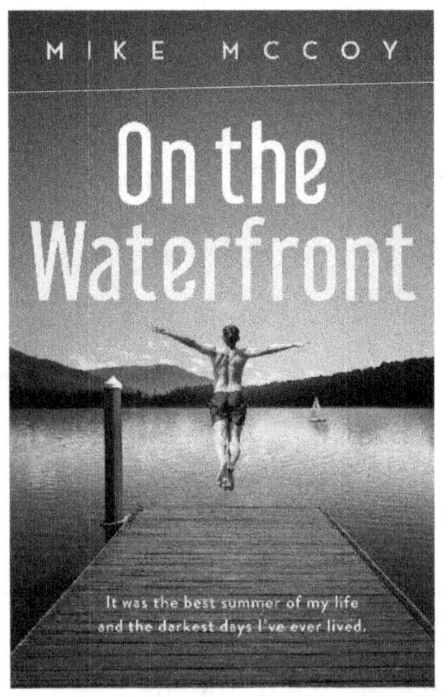

It was the best summer of his life, and the darkest days he ever lived.

Danny Novak, at thirteen, was hired to work at Camp Baker for the summer. He's the youngest boy on staff, but he's sure he'll fit right in. He quickly learns, it's not that easy. When Danny fails the swim test to work on the waterfront, Mark, the bad boy on staff, is forced to teach Danny to swim or get sent home. Home is the last place Mark wants to go, but he wants nothing to do with the skinny little runt who's ruined his summer. Mark forces Danny to swim, but even if he passes the test, will the other guys on the waterfront accept him?
On the Waterfront is a bittersweet coming of age tale of two boys struggling for acceptance and friendship.

A surprising summer camp tale of unlikely friendships and young adulthood.
McCoy writes with passion, illuminating the angst of young males trying to find their footing, and his characters are as believable as they are entertaining.

The jolting conclusion invites picking back through the novel, reading again in a new light, but the book's heart isn't just in its surprise. McCoy evokes those muggy summer nights of cricket chirping and self-discovery that will resonate with readers of character-driven literary fiction. **Publishers Weekly - Book Life Reviews**

"On the Waterfront is comedic and heartbreaking, sharing the experiences of a young man trying to grow up on his own. The author has a conversational and engaging style, a deeply personal tone, easy pacing, and good character development. On the Waterfront is a sentimental, sometimes funny, poignant, and bittersweet novel, which makes it an entertaining and memorable read. If you are a fan of the coming-of-age genre, this book is for you." **Readers Favorite**

"A classic coming-of-age story. Danny is an endearing, often funny voice, and his struggles are evocatively drawn. This may be a story about the small moments that shape a life, but McCoy imbues his story with relatable emotion and pathos. Danny is a wholly captivating lead character, and readers will quickly embrace his story as he navigates the rites of passage that yield profound revelations about friendship, power, fear, and what it means to grow up." **Self-Publishing Review**

About the Author

Mike McCoy is an international businessman and entrepreneur who has traveled extensively and worked in the consumer electronics industry for over twenty-five years. The company he founded developed a variety of innovative products which sold in retail stores around the world. Mike is also an accomplished athlete known for long distance events. He completed a full Ironman Triathlon in 2006. He thought running fifty miles would be a good accomplishment, so for his fiftieth birthday he ran a double Marathon (52.4 miles). In 2018, Mike celebrated his sixtieth birthday with a six-hundred-mile bike ride from Florence, Oregon to San Francisco, California. Somehow, he finds time to write.

Check Mike's website and Facebook page for news and updates:
www.MikeMcCoy.me
www.facebook.com/AuthorMikeMcCoy